I SPY
NUMBERS

Rhymes by Jean Marzollo

Photographs by Walter Wick

With thanks to Sandra Nice and Nice Care, Inc.

ISBN 978-0-545-41585-9

I Spy Numbers was originally published as a board book
under the title *I Spy Little Numbers*.

Text copyright © 1999 by Jean Marzollo.
"1, 2, 3..." from *I Spy School Days* © 1995 by Walter Wick, published by Scholastic Inc.

10 9 8 7 6 5 4 3 2   12 13 14 15 16

Printed in the U.S.A. 40 • This edition first printing, January 2012

I SPY

NUMBERS

Rhymes by Jean Marzollo

Photographs by Walter Wick

Cartwheel
·B·O·O·K·S·®

SCHOLASTIC INC.
New York   Toronto   London   Auckland
Sydney   Mexico City   New Delhi   Hong Kong

I spy a hot dog in a bun,

a teddy bear,

and a big red one.

I spy a great big yellow two,

a pair of scissors,

and a button that's blue.

I spy a bright green number three.

How many piggy-wiggies can you see?

I spy a four,

and a yellow van,

 a spotted frog,

and a raincoat man.

I spy a five,

 a little airplane,

a soccer ball,

 and a choo-choo train.

I spy a six,

 a small guitar, too;

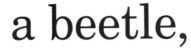 a beetle,

and a bow on a yellow shoe.

I spy a seven,

 two dominoes with dots,

a yellow flower,

 and a cow with spots.

I spy a spider,

 a red race car,

a big blue eight,

and an 8-pointed star.

I spy a ball,

9 a nine that's red,

and a baseball player

with a cap on his head.

When you are done, go back and look...

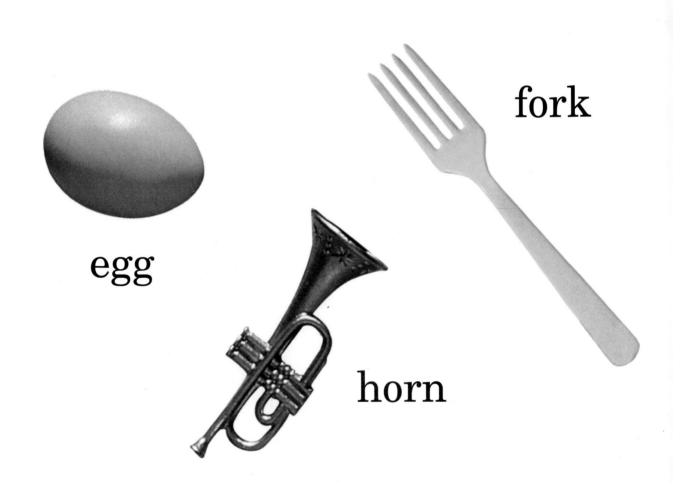

egg

horn

fork

What else can you find in your I Spy book?

peas in a pod

tomato top

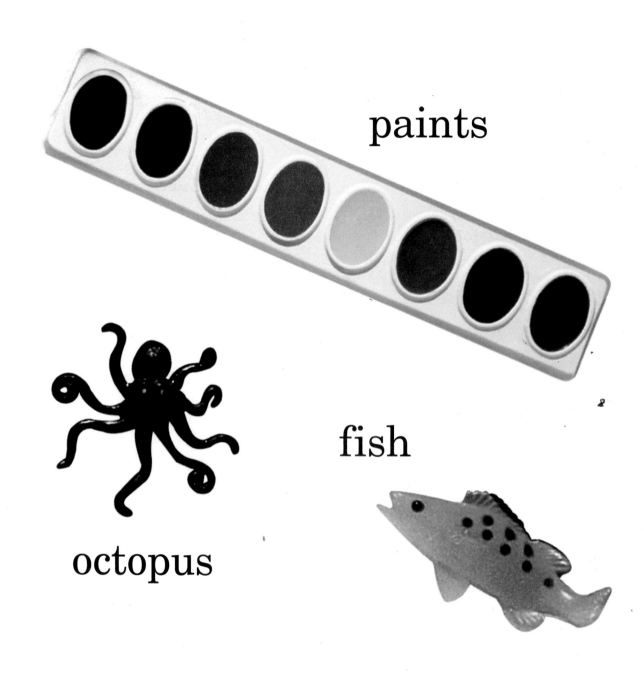

paints

octopus

fish

spaghetti wheel

crown

broom

bicycle

dinosaur

sunglasses

When you are done,
go back and look.

1 2 3 4 5
6 7 8 9

Can you find these numbers
in your I Spy book?

Collect the I Spy books

Classics

Collect the I Spy books

Challengers

Also available are *I Spy A to Z*, *I Spy Spectacular*, I Spy early readers,
I Spy Little board books, and *I Spy Phonics Fun*.

Find all the I Spy books and more at www.scholastic.com/ispy/.